THE GINGERBREAD MAN

and other stories

Retold by

MARY HOFFMAN

Illustrated by

ANNA CURREY

MACMILLAN
CHILDREN'S BOOKS

First published in 2000 in *The Macmillan Treasury of Nursery Stories.*
This collection published in 2001 by Macmillan Children's Books
A division of Macmillan Publishers Limited
25 Eccleston Place, London SW1W 9NF,
Basingstoke and Oxford
Associated companies throughout the world.
www.macmillan.com

ISBN 0 333 96131 5

1 3 5 7 9 8 6 4 2

Printed in Hong Kong

Contents

The Gingerbread Man

Once upon a time a farmer's wife made a batch of gingerbread and with a leftover piece she shaped a little man. You might not think this unusual, because you can see gingerbread men in any baker's window, but this one was the very first such man that had ever been made.

The farmer's wife gave him raisins for eyes and, when he was baked and cooled, she took her icing bag and gave him a bow tie, a mouth and three buttons down his front.

"What a handsome fellow you are!" she exclaimed. "It will be a shame to eat you."

"Eat me!" cried the gingerbread man, sitting up on the baking tray. "No fear—I'm off!"

And he jumped off the table and ran out of the kitchen door. At first the farmer's wife was too astonished to move but, when she saw her sweet treat running away, she set off after him. But he just called out:

"Run, run, fast as you can,

You can't catch me—I'm the Gingerbread Man!"

He had soon put the farm far behind him and found himself in a village. He was running past the butcher's shop when the butcher caught sight of him.

"Stop, let me eat you," cried the butcher.

But the gingerbread man just kept running, calling back over his shoulder:

"Run, run, fast as you can,

You can't catch me—I'm the Gingerbread Man!"

He ran past the blacksmith's and the blacksmith himself came out to look. When he saw the gingerbread man, his mouth watered and he gave chase. But the little man ran on, crying:

"Run, run, fast as you can,
You can't catch me—I'm
the Gingerbread Man!"

A little while later he came to the flour mill and the miller ran out to catch him. "Stop, stop!" cried the miller, "I want to eat you up!"

Well, of course, that made the
gingerbread man run faster, calling out:

"Run, run, fast as you can,

You can't catch me—I'm the Gingerbread Man!"

By now he was outside the village and running across
a field, where he was spotted by a very surprised cow.
He nearly ran into her mouth as she munched the grass.
She caught a whiff of his delicious smell and started to
lumber after him, mooing in such a way that he knew
what she intended.

So he ran even faster, crying out to the cow:

"Run, run, fast as you can,

You can't catch me—I'm the Gingerbread Man!"

Now he was in the horse's field and the horse came to

investigate him. "Neigh!" said the horse. "You look tasty. Stop and let me try you."

So the gingerbread man started to sprint, crying:

"Run, run, fast as you can,
You can't catch me—
I'm the Gingerbread Man!"
Suddenly, he realised that he could go no further. There was a stream at the bottom of the field and the horse was behind him. But there was a handsome red fox grooming himself on the bank of the stream and he offered to ferry the gingerbread man across.

The fox was the only being the gingerbread man had met that morning who hadn't wanted to eat him, so he took hold of the fox's tail and the fox started to swim across the stream. Halfway across he said to the gingerbread man, "I am afraid you will get wet. Climb onto my back." So the gingerbread man did.

Three quarters of the way across the stream, the fox said, "I am still afraid you will get wet. Why not climb onto my head?" So the gingerbread man did.

And when they were nearly at the opposite bank, the fox said, "This is the awkward bit. When I get out of the water I have to shake my fur. If you climb onto my nose you will stay dry."

So the gingerbread man climbed onto the fox's nose.

And then the fox flipped up his long red nose, opened his big greedy mouth and swallowed the gingerbread man up in one bite!

And that was the end of the first gingerbread man. Many of them have been made and eaten since and I shouldn't wonder if you've had one yourself.

Snow White

Once upon a time a beautiful queen sat sewing at her window. It was winter and her ebony window framed a landscape all white with snow. The queen pricked her finger and, as the bright blood welled up, she thought, "How I wish I had a little girl whose skin was as white as snow, whose hair was as black as ebony and whose lips were as red as this blood!"

And, by the end of the year, the queen's wish came true,

for she gave birth to a baby girl, whose skin was as white
as snow, her hair black as ebony and her lips red as blood.
But it was a hard birth and the queen died of it. The king
was very sad and he called his little daughter Snow White.

Time went by and the king was lonely, so he married
again. His second wife was a beauty, too, but a very vain
one. She had a magic mirror in her bedchamber and
every morning she spoke to it:

"Mirror, mirror, on the wall,
Who is the fairest one of all?"

And the mirror would reply:

"The loveliest creature ever seen
Is none but you, O gracious queen!"

The queen was not fond of Snow
White, who grew prettier with every
day. So imagine her shock when, one
day, she asked her mirror, "Who is the fairest one of all?"
and heard this reply:

"She who makes the darkness bright,
The lovely princess called Snow White."

The queen was furious, but she knew that the mirror never lied. So she made a terrible plan. She called the palace's chief huntsman to her and told him to take the child into the forest and kill her.

"And when you've done it, bring me her lungs and liver as proof!" said the wicked queen.

The huntsman went to call Snow White to join him for a walk in the forest. She went with him happily because she knew all the people who worked in the palace and they were all nice to her. As they got deeper among the trees, the huntsman thought he really couldn't kill the sweet, pretty girl. So he told her about the queen's orders. "Run away, Snow White," he said, "and God keep you safe."

But he secretly thought she would probably be killed by wild beasts anyway.

As he travelled back to the palace, the huntsman killed a wild boar and took its lungs and liver to the queen.

"So, it is done," she said. "Tell the cook I'll have them for supper."

Snow White was very scared alone in the forest. But no animals harmed her and, in the end, she came to a little cottage with smoke coming out of the chimney, 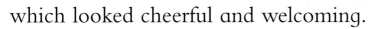 which looked cheerful and welcoming.

There was no one at home, but Snow White had to rest, so she went in. There was a wooden table set with seven little plates, seven little mugs and seven little knives and forks. There was food on the plates and wine in the mugs and Snow White was so hungry that she took a little bread and vegetable from each plate and a sip of wine from each mug, so that it wouldn't be missed all at once.

Then she saw seven little beds lined up against the wall. She was so tired that she wanted to go to sleep in one of them, but one was too short, one too soft and one too lumpy. She tried them all and the seventh one seemed the most comfortable, so she snuggled under the covers and fell fast asleep.

When it grew dark, the owners of the house came home. They were seven dwarves, who worked in the mines all day, digging out copper and gold. As soon as they got inside they knew someone had touched their meal and they could see dents in their beds. But the seventh dwarf found a little girl fast asleep in his!

The dwarves gathered round to admire the sleeping child. They were kindly creatures and thought they had never seen anything so lovely as Snow White. At that moment, she woke up and saw seven little faces with white beards, looking down at her. She told them her story, about how her stepmother had wanted to kill her and how she had run away.

"That's all right, my dear," said the dwarves. "You'll be safe with us, as long as you don't let anyone into the house. You can stay here and we'll look after you but, in return, you must do all the cooking and cleaning and tidying of the house."

"I'd like that," said Snow White.

When they had eaten their supper, they went to bed and the seventh dwarf slept one hour in each of the other dwarves' beds so that Snow White could have his.

Back at the palace the next morning, the queen asked her mirror:

"Mirror, mirror, on the wall,
  Who is the fairest one of all?"

But the mirror replied:

"O Queen, you are fairest of all I see,
  But over the hills, where the seven dwarves dwell,
  Snow White is still alive and well,
  And none is as fair as she."

Then the queen knew she had been tricked and plotted even harder to get rid of Snow White. She disguised herself as a pedlar-woman and went to the dwarves' cottage.

Snow White was happily dusting and sweeping while the dwarves were at the mines, when she heard a voice calling, "See my lovely ribbons and laces. Pretty things for pretty girls." Snow White couldn't resist and she opened the door. The pedlar-woman stepped in and said, "Wouldn't you like to buy yourself something nice as a treat after all your housework? How about this lace?"

And she showed Snow White a rainbow-coloured lace for her bodice. "Here, let me thread it for you," said the old woman, and she laced Snow White so tightly into her bodice that she couldn't breathe and fell down on the floor.

When the dwarves came home they thought their little friend was dead. But they quickly cut the rainbow lace and Snow White could breathe again. She told them what had happened. "But that must have been the wicked queen," they said. "You must be on your guard and not let anyone in the house."

Back at the palace, the queen asked the mirror her usual question. But the answer came:

"While Snow White breathes and shows her worth,
  She's still the fairest on this earth."

The queen ground her teeth with rage and thought how she might kill her enemy. She knew all sorts of witchcraft and disguised herself again to look like a quite different old woman. Then she put poison on a hair comb and set out for the dwarves' cottage.

Snow White was baking an apple pie when she heard a voice saying, "Who would like something pretty for her hair?" Snow White opened the door and saw an old woman with a tray full of bows and slides and pretty combs.

"I know just the thing for you," said the old woman, holding out the poisoned comb. "Just think how these sparkling stones will set off your dark hair."

And Snow White was so fond of sparkly things that she let the pedlar in.

The old woman showed her the comb and put it in her hair. Immediately, the poison entered Snow White's skin and she fell down in a swoon. But luckily it was nearly time for the dwarves to come home and, as soon as they found her, they drew the comb out of her hair.

Snow White sat up, well as ever and anxious to get her pie in the oven. But the dwarves were very worried. "You really must promise not to open the door to anyone," they told her. "The queen is determined to kill you."

Back at the palace, the queen spoke to her mirror and it said:

"The loveliest creature alive tonight
  Is the beautiful princess called Snow White."

The queen tore her hair with fury. She used all her witchcraft to make a poisoned apple. It was red on one side and white on the other and looked as tasty as an apple can be, but one bite from the red side was deadly. Then the queen turned herself into a farmer's wife and went to the dwarves' cottage.

Snow White was making a pair of curtains when she heard a voice call, "Apples, apples, nice sweet apples!"

Now, Snow White was very
fond of apples, but she knew
she mustn't open the door.
So she opened the window
instead. How delicious the
apple looked that the farmer's
wife was holding out to her!

"Apple, my pretty?" asked the old woman.

Snow White shook her black hair. "I'm not allowed,"
she said.

"Why ever not?" said the old woman. "They're good
and wholesome. Look, I'll take a bite myself." And she bit
out some juicy flesh from the white side of the apple.
Then she held out the red side to Snow White. The little
girl couldn't help herself. She took a bite.

Immediately, Snow White fell down dead and the
witch queen ran happily back to the palace. When the
dwarves came home, they could not revive Snow White.
They looked for laces and combs but didn't think to look
inside her mouth. Sadly, they agreed that she must be
dead, but she still looked so beautiful that they couldn't
bear to bury her. So they made a glass coffin and
put Snow White in it, and put it on a hilltop nearby.

One of the dwarves watched over the coffin every day.

The queen was happy at last in her palace, for whenever she asked the mirror,

"Mirror, mirror, on the wall,
  Who is the fairest one of all?"

it replied:

"The loveliest creature ever seen
  Is none but you, O gracious queen."

And she was very happy that her rival was dead at last.

As for the dwarves, they missed Snow White very much. She didn't change a bit, keeping her rosy cheeks and her white complexion. Years went by and, one day, a young king was out hunting in the hills. He saw the glass coffin and immediately fell in love with the beautiful girl who seemed to be sleeping in it. He spoke to the dwarf who was on guard by the coffin and heard the whole of Snow White's story.

The king begged and pleaded with the dwarves to let him take the glass coffin back to his kingdom, so that he could continue to gaze at the girl. He offered them a large heap of gold in return. At first they wouldn't hear of it, but he seemed so broken-hearted that eventually they said yes.

The king had the coffin put on a carriage pulled by horses but as they set off through the forest, the first horse stumbled on a tree root. The coffin slipped off and fell on the ground, tipping Snow White out. And, with that, the piece of poisoned apple was dislodged from her mouth. She woke and found herself looking into the eyes of a handsome young man.

In a moment the king was on his knees asking Snow White to marry him, and she was happy to say yes. She said goodbye to the seven dwarves and went to live with her king in his kingdom.

The invitations soon went out to a grand wedding.

Now, when Snow White's wicked stepmother got her invitation, she spent days getting herself ready. When she was dressed in all her finery, the wicked queen asked her mirror:

"Mirror, mirror, on the wall,
    Who is the fairest one of all?"

and got this reply:

"Of all ladies here you the loveliest are,
    But the new young queen is fairer by far."

The queen turned pale with fury. But she was even more furious when she arrived at the wedding and saw that the bride was Snow White! She was so angry that she couldn't move. All her magic froze up inside her and she turned to stone.

Snow White lived happily with her king and she had the wicked queen moved to the park where she made a beautiful statue for the birds to sit on.

The Princess
and the Pea

There was once a prince who decided he must have a wife, but the only wife that would do for him was what he called "a real princess". However, he didn't seem at all sure what that meant. Still, as he searched for one, he became more certain about who was *not* a real princess.

The prince travelled from country to country and found lots of princesses but there was always something wrong with them. One was too tall, one had bandy legs, one ate nothing but salad, one had a passion for wearing yellow, one beat her servants, one read nothing but romantic novels.

It seemed as if there was not one princess in this world good enough to marry the prince and he went back to his own castle very disappointed.

Then, one night, there was a terrible storm, with thunder and lightning and torrential rain. And at the height of the storm there came a knocking at the castle door. The servant who opened it found a very bedraggled young woman on the doorstep. Her clothes stuck to her body and water ran down her pretty face and hair in streams.

"Please give me shelter," she said. "And, by the way, I am a real princess."

Everyone in the castle had come to see who was at the door on such an awful night. There she stood, calm and dignified and sopping wet. "Can this be a real princess?" wondered the prince.

His mother, the queen, had an idea of her own about that. "Come in and warm yourself, my dear," she said, and ordered servants to prepare her a hot bath and fetch her dry clothes. And while all this was going on, the queen had the best guest bedroom prepared in a most unusual way.

The bed was stripped and one dried pea placed on the bedstead. Then twenty mattresses were piled on top of it and cotton sheets and a big fluffy duck-down duvet. If the princess thought her bed at all odd when she came to get in it, she said nothing. She merely climbed the handy ladder that had been provided and settled down to sleep.

The next morning the princess appeared at breakfast with dark circles under her eyes.

"How did you sleep?" asked the queen.

"Very badly, ma'am," said the princess. "I'm sorry to say it but my bed was very uncomfortable. I felt there was something hard and sharp underneath me and I tossed and turned all night."

"A real princess at last!" cried the prince, clapping his hands. "Only a royal lady of the utmost refinement could have felt that pea under twenty mattresses."

And he went down on one knee and asked her to marry him on the spot. Perhaps it was lucky for him that she was not searching for a perfect prince. Anyway, what is certain is that marry they did, and they lived together all the days of their lives. And the pea was preserved in a glass case in a museum and, if it is still there, you may see it to this day.

The Musicians
of Bremen

There was once a donkey who had worked all his life for a miller but was now getting old. He knew that the miller couldn't afford to keep him as a pet so he decided to set out for the town of Bremen and become a musician there. After all, he could sing a fine "hee-haw!"

On his way he met a dog, lying by the side of the road and panting. "What's the matter?" asked the donkey.

"I've run away from home," said the dog. "I am too old

to hunt any more and I think my master was planning to shoot me."

"Then why not come with me?" said the donkey. "I'm going to Bremen to be a musician. You could do that, too. You know how to howl, I suppose?"

When the dog had recovered, the two new friends walked on towards Bremen. After a short while they came across a cat sitting on the path looking very sorry for itself.

"What's the matter?" they asked.

"My teeth are not as sharp as they were and I've lost the taste for catching mice, so my mistress has thrown me out."

"Then come with us to Bremen," said the donkey and the dog. "We are going to be musicians and you could join us. We know how tunefully cats sing at night."

Not long after this the three companions passed a farm and there sat a cock on the gatepost, crowing with all his might.

"It's not morning," said the other animals. "Why are you crowing now?"

"I heard my mistress say I was getting too old. I am supposed to be turned into stew tomorrow, so I'm singing as much as I can today."

"Well, bring your fine singing voice to Bremen with us," said the others. "Wouldn't you rather be a musician than end up in the pot?"

The cock agreed and the four friends went on their way. When night fell, they settled in a wood. The donkey and the dog lay at the foot of a tree, while the cat climbed up into its branches and the cock flew right to the top.

While he was up there, the cock saw a distant light. He flew down to tell his friends.

"I think there's a house over there. Perhaps we could find better lodging and maybe some food?"

So they set off towards the light. It came from a very cosy house on the edge of the wood. The donkey, being the tallest, looked in at the window and came back to tell them what he had seen.

"It's a robbers' house," he said. "They are all sitting round a table and it is absolutely loaded with good things to eat and drink."

So the four friends made a plan. The donkey went back to the window and the dog climbed up on his back and the cat sat on the dog's shoulders, while the cock perched on the cat's head. Then they gave their first concert.

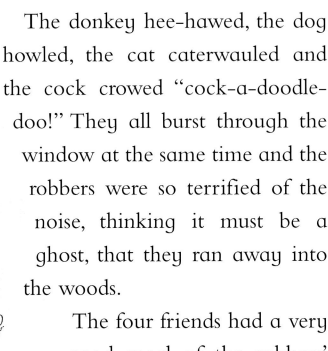

The donkey hee-hawed, the dog howled, the cat caterwauled and the cock crowed "cock-a-doodle-doo!" They all burst through the window at the same time and the robbers were so terrified of the noise, thinking it must be a ghost, that they ran away into the woods.

The four friends had a very good meal of the robbers' food and then settled down to sleep in the places that suited them best. The donkey lay on some straw in the yard. The dog slept behind the door, the cat curled up near the remains of the fire and the cock flew up into the rafters.

The robbers began to get over their fright and sent one member of the gang back to the house to see what was going on. In he crept, but the house was in darkness now, so he thought he would light a taper at the fire. He mistook the cat's eyes for two burning coals and poked the taper at them.

The cat shrieked and flew at the man's face, scratching him with its claws. He stumbled over the dog by the door, who bit him in the leg. He ran out into the yard, where the donkey kicked him hard and the cock flew down from the rafters crowing "cock-a-doodle-doo!"

The robber got back to his friends in a terrible state.

"There's a dreadful witch in the house," he cried. "She scratched me and cursed me. And then a man with a knife stabbed me in the leg as I was coming out of the door and a monster was waiting in the yard, who beat me with a wooden club! And then a judge called from up on the roof—'There's nothing you can do!'—so I ran away as fast as I could."

When his companions saw the robber's scratches and bruises, no one dared go back to the house. So the four friends lived there in happiness to the end of their days and never reached Bremen at all.

The Three Heads
in the Well

Long ago in England, well before the time of good King Arthur and his knights, there reigned a king in Colchester. He had a lovely queen who died, leaving him the care of their fifteen-year-old daughter. The king was a bit short of money, so he married a rich widow who was very ugly and who had a daughter as unattractive as herself.

Now, the new queen was jealous of the king's pretty

daughter and planned to turn him against her. She made up lots of horrid stories about the princess, and she was so successful that the king believed her and told his daughter that she must leave home and go to seek her own fortune in the world.

So off she was sent, with nothing but a canvas sack with some brown bread and hard cheese in it, and a bottle of beer. The young princess said thank you for the food and then travelled along the road till she came to a cave, with an old man sitting outside it.

"Where are you going, pretty maid?" he asked.

"To seek my fortune," said the princess.

"And what is in your bag and bottle?"

"Just bread and cheese and beer," said the princess, "but you are welcome to share it."

So they divided the little picnic and the princess kept her half for later. When the old man had finished eating, he gave the princess a wand and said, "You will soon come to a thorny hedge, but just tap it with this wand and you will pass through safely. Then you will see a well with three golden heads in it. Do whatever they ask you, and you will be rewarded."

The princess thanked him and went on her way. She came to the high thorny hedge and tapped it with the wand.

Straight away, the hedge parted and she could walk through without a scratch. On the other side was a well.

When the princess approached it, up bobbed a golden head, singing this song:

"Wash me and comb me
And lay me down gently,
Put me on the bank to dry
So I may look pretty
To those who pass by."

The princess was very surprised, but she lifted the head gently out of the well and washed its face carefully and combed its tangled hair with a little silver comb she had brought in her pocket. Then she laid the head down on the grass to dry.

Two more heads popped up, one at a time and sang the same little song. Twice more the princess washed and combed them and, when all three heads lay on the grass, she sat down and ate her lunch.

The three heads talked to one another:
"What shall we give this girl who has been so kind
to us?"

The first one said,
"She shall stay as beautiful as
she is today and win the
heart of a great prince."

The second one said,
"She shall have a voice
as sweet as a nightingale's."

And the third said, "She is
the daughter of a king and shall
be a greater ruler than he."

When the princess had finished her food, she said
goodbye to the golden heads and went on her way.

Before long, she met a handsome young king out riding with his dogs. He fell in love with her beautiful face and kind ways and they were soon married.

The young king discovered that his beautiful wife was the daughter of the King of Colchester and said that they must go and visit him. Imagine how surprised the old king was to see his daughter coming back dressed in silks and lace and wearing expensive jewels!

Her husband told his father-in-law all about the heads in the well and the ugly queen overheard him. "It's not fair how well that girl has done for herself!" she protested. "My daughter must have the same chances."

So she sent for her own daughter and gave her a velvet bag with roast chicken and sugared almonds and a bottle of sweet wine and sent her out on the same road the other princess had taken.

But this was a very different sort of girl. When she met the old man at the cave, he said, "Where are you going, young woman?" and she replied, "Mind your own business!"

"What have you in your bag and bottle?" asked the old man.

"All manner of good things," said the rude girl, "but you're not getting any."

When she came to the thorny hedge, the girl saw a gap she thought she could climb through. But, as soon as she tried to pass, the hedge closed up and pricked her skin with a thousand thorns.

Once she was through, the girl was bleeding from all her scratches and in a very bad mood, as you may imagine. She flounced over to the well to clean off the blood and saw a golden head sitting in it.

"Wash me and comb me
     And lay me down gently,
     Put me on the bank to dry
     So I may look pretty
     To those who pass by."

sang the head.

"Take that!" said the girl and banged the head with her bottle. The two other heads fared no better. The grumpy girl sat on the grass and ate her delicious lunch. Meanwhile, the heads asked one another, "What shall we do for this horrible girl?"

The first one said, "I'll curse her face with an ugly rash."

The second one said, "I wish her a voice as harsh as a corncrake's."

And the third one said, "I wish her a poor country cobbler for a husband."

When the girl had finished her lunch, she went on her way and reached a village. All the villagers ran screaming when they saw her face all covered with spots and heard her harsh voice. The only person who stayed was the cobbler.

He had recently mended some shoes for a poor hermit, who had paid him with a special ointment to cure skin rashes and a potion to cure a harsh voice. He felt sorry for the girl and asked her who she was.

"I am the King of Colchester's stepdaughter," she said, though by now she wasn't quite as proud as before.

"Then, if I heal your face and your voice," said the cobbler, "will you marry me?"

The girl had been so upset when everyone ran away from her that she said yes.

So she married the cobbler and they went to visit the court at Colchester. The girl's mother was so disgusted that she had married a cobbler that she refused to talk to her, but the king was highly amused. He paid the cobbler a hundred pounds.

So the ugly girl and the cobbler lived together quite comfortably and, if they weren't quite as happy as the pretty girl and her king, they weren't much less so, for the girl had learned her lesson and was a much nicer person than when she met the three heads in the well.

The
Country Mouse and
the City Mouse

There were once two mice who were good friends. One was a house mouse who lived in a big city and the other was a field mouse who lived in the countryside.

The city mouse paid his friend a visit in the country and the field mouse was very glad to see him.

"Come with me and we will have a feast of ripe barley and wheat," he said.

The city mouse ate a good dinner but he didn't seem satisfied.

"Ah," he sighed. "You should see what I get to eat in the town—cheese, figs, honey, sultanas, apples. You would soon tire of all this field-food if you tasted city life. Why don't you come and stay with me so I can show you?"

So the country mouse went home with his friend. He was very frightened by all the many pairs of feet and carriage wheels on the street and very relieved when they reached the city mouse's house.

As soon as the city mouse had shown his friend his comfortable home behind the skirting board, they set out to find their dinner.

"You see how conveniently my home is situated," boasted the city mouse. "In the kitchen, the best room in all the house."

He led his friend through a tiny crack at the bottom of a door into a larder, where there were the most delicious smells.

The little country mouse's mouth watered. They scampered up onto a high shelf where there sat a tasty cheese. But no sooner had they started to nibble the edges off it than a large person opened the larder door and reached for the shelf!

The mice scuttled away and hid. When all was quiet again they came out and this time climbed onto the kitchen table. In the middle of it was a handsome cake, made with sultanas and cherries and many other kinds of dried fruit. The country mouse's whiskers twitched. This was finer fare than he ever found in a field.

But they had not tasted more than a crumb of the cake's icing before someone else came into the room and they had to run and hide again. Back in the city mouse's hole, the country mouse gasped for breath, his little heart pounding.

"You can keep your fine city food," he panted. "I grant you it is very fine indeed and probably delicious but you have to put up with so many dangers to get it that, as for me, I would rather eat the humble grains I find in the fields than risk so much to get fancier meals."

And he headed back to the country where he lived happily for the rest of his days, though he never tasted cake. And the city mouse lived happily, too, because he was used to the dangers of his way of life and much too fond of cake to leave it behind.

The Wolf and
the Seven Little Kids

There was once a nanny goat who had seven little kids, whom she loved as dearly as any human mother ever loved her babies. One day she had to go into the forest to fetch some food, but she was worried about a wolf who lived nearby. So she called all her seven children to her and gave them some advice.

"My dear little kids, I must go and get us some food. Now while I am away, you must watch out for the wolf.

He is very good at disguises, but you should know him by his rough voice and his black feet."

"Don't worry, Mother," said the kids. "We will take care of one another."

So away she went. Not long afterwards someone came to the door and knocked, saying, "Let me in, dear little kids. It is your mother come back and I have something nice for each of you to eat."

But it was a harsh rough voice and the little kids bleated, "You are not our mother! She has a soft gentle voice and yours is so horrid you must be the wolf!"

The wolf went to a shop and bought himself a huge pot of honey. He ate the lot and it made his voice soft and pleasant. Then he went back to the goats' house and knocked on the door, saying, "Dear little kids, let me in. It is I, your mother, and I have something nice for each of you to eat."

But while he was talking, the wolf laid his black paws against the window and the kids cried out, "You are not our mother! She has sweet white woolly feet. Yours are so hairy and black, you must be the wolf!"

Cursing and growling, the wolf ran to the mill and told

the miller to sprinkle his paws with white flour. At first the miller said no, guessing the wolf was trying to deceive someone. But the wolf threatened to eat him if he didn't, so the miller sprinkled the wolf's paws with flour.

A third time the wolf came to the goats' house and called, "Dear little kids, let me in. It is I, your mother, and I have something nice for each of you to eat."

"Show us your feet," said the kids.

And the wolf obligingly put his floury paws on the window sill. The kids were quite convinced it was their mother this time and opened the door. Whoosh! In rushed the wolf, and the kids all scattered. One hid under the table, one in the bed, one inside the stove, one in a cupboard, one behind the woodpile and  one inside the washing bowl. The seventh and youngest little kid hid inside the case of the grandfather clock.

The wolf found them all except the seventh and ate them all up.

Not long afterwards the nanny goat came home. How upset she was to see the door open, the table knocked on its side and the washing bowl broken on the floor. She ran about the house distracted with worry, calling her kids by name. But it wasn't until she called the seventh one that she heard any reply. "Is that you, Mother?" called the frightened little kid from inside the grandfather clock.

How she embraced her one remaining child, weeping as she heard what had happened to the other six. In her grief she wandered out of the house, with the last little kid trotting behind her, and strayed into a nearby meadow.

There they found the wolf sleeping off his huge meal. The poor goat saw something squirming in his stomach and thought, "Could it be that my children are still alive?" She sent the littlest kid back to the house to fetch a knife and a needle and strong thread. When he got back, the goat cut open the wolf's stomach. He had been so greedy that he had swallowed the six little kids whole! One by one they came popping out of the cut that their mother had made.

What rejoicing there was when the mother and her

precious children were reunited! The wolf slept on and while he snored, the kids found some big stones and put them in his stomach and the goat sewed him up again with the needle and thread. Then the goat and the seven little kids went and hid behind a tree to see what would happen.

When the wolf woke up he felt terribly thirsty but, as he walked towards the stream to quench his thirst, the stones in his stomach knocked together and made him feel very peculiar.

When he reached the stream, the wolf put his head down to drink and the weight of the stones unbalanced him so that he fell into the water and drowned.

As soon as the seven little kids saw what had happened to the wolf, they danced for joy, singing:

"The wolf is gone, the wolf is drowned,
The kids he ate have all been found.
The wolf is drowned, the wolf is dead
We'll eat our supper and go to bed!"

Jack and the Beanstalk

There was once a widow who had one son, called Jack. He was the apple of her eye but he was an idle, thoughtless fellow. He spent his mother's money carelessly so that, in time, it ran out and they had nothing left but their one cow.

"It's no good, Jack," said his mother. "We will have to sell the cow if we are to have anything to eat. You must drive her to market and be sure to get a good price for her."

"All right, Mother," said Jack. "You can trust me."

And he set off to market with the cow. But, on his way, he met a man who had some curious coloured beans in his hat. The man saw that they had attracted Jack's attention and asked him where he was going with his cow.

"Why, to market," said Jack. "I am going to sell her."

"Well, why don't you save yourself a journey and sell her to me for these five beans," said the man. "They're magic beans, you know."

Jack thought that his mother would be glad to see him back so soon and the cow sold so easily, so the foolish boy exchanged the good milking cow for a handful of beans.

And was his mother pleased? She was not. In fact, for the first time in his life she flew into a temper with Jack and boxed his ears!

"Stupid boy!" she scolded. "Now what are we to live on? Magic beans, indeed—let's see if they fill your belly tonight!"

And she threw the beans out of the window. Jack went to bed supperless and very miserable; he was not used to being in his mother's bad books.

Next morning, when he looked out of the window, he couldn't believe his eyes. A huge beanstalk had grown up, higher than the house. In fact, it was so high, no one could see the top of it. In spite of his mother's fears and warnings, Jack decided he would climb it and see what was at the top. So he climbed and climbed, until he was sure he must reach the sky. After some hours, he arrived at the top and found himself in a strange country. It was very desolate, with nothing but rocks and boulders around.

Jack could see a big house in the distance and he set off towards it. It loomed bigger and bigger as he got near it, for it was, in fact, a giant's house. Jack clambered up the huge steps to the door. The giant wasn't at home, but his wife answered Jack's knock at the door. He asked her for food and drink but she told him to go away. "You will be in great danger when my husband comes back," she said. "He eats human beings and he'd make short work of you."

But Jack begged and pleaded and, in the end, she let him in and gave him something to eat, and then hid him inside the stove. Just in time, for the giant was coming back and Jack could hear his mighty footsteps rumbling up the stairs.

When the giant came into the kitchen, he looked round suspiciously, sniffing the air, and said,

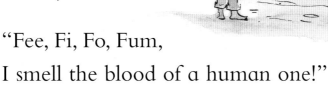

"Fee, Fi, Fo, Fum,
I smell the blood of a human one!"

But his wife persuaded him that it was just his supper chops he could smell. (Wasn't it lucky that she was frying them on top of the stove and not roasting them inside it?) Jack was quivering with fear in his hiding place.

The giant ate thirty-six huge chops for supper and twenty pounds of potatoes. Jack thought he would never stop. Then the giant called for his wife to bring him his pet hen. Jack couldn't believe how gentle and kind the horrible giant was to the little hen. But then she laid an egg—of pure gold! Now Jack could see why the giant was so fond of her.

It wasn't long before the giant was asleep and snoring. Jack crept out of the stove, snatched up the hen and ran out of the giant's house.

He didn't stop running till he reached the top of the beanstalk and climbed awkwardly down it, with the hen under his arm.

His mother was waiting anxiously for him at the bottom of the beanstalk.

"See, Mother," said Jack. "I am not good for nothing. I have brought you a hen to replace the cow."

"Well," said his mother, "it will be good to have eggs to eat even if we have no milk to drink."

"These eggs are not for eating," said Jack, and he set the little hen gently down on the ground, where she laid an egg of solid gold.

Jack and his mother lived very well after that, selling the golden eggs. Their larder was always full and they bought themselves another cow and some ordinary hens.

But Jack could never forget his adventure up the beanstalk, of which he had said little to his mother, as she tended to worry about him. As the months went by, he felt more and more restless and eventually he just had to go back up it again.

His mother tried to stop him, but it was no good. He disguised himself, in case the giant's wife should recognise him, and set off on his long climb.

The country was just as before and he made his way back to the giant's house and knocked at the door. The giant's wife didn't recognise him but she refused to let him in.

"Not long ago I took pity on a poor lad like you and he stole my husband's magic hen," said the giantess, "and now I never hear the end of it."

But Jack flattered and cajoled her and, in the end, she let him in and fed him and hid him in a cupboard. Not much later, Jack heard the sounds of the giant returning.

"Fee, Fi, Fo, Fum,

I smell the blood of a human one,"

said the giant, sniffing the air.

"Nay, it is nothing but the side of beef I am roasting for your supper," said the giantess.

Jack watched through a crack in the cupboard door while the giant ate the whole side of beef and three apple pies, each the size of a dustbin lid. All the time he was eating, the giant was grumbling to his wife about the loss of his hen.

After his supper, the giant called for something to amuse him and his wife brought him his sacks of money to count, which was a favourite hobby of the giant's. Jack's eyes nearly popped out of his head when he saw how many silver pieces spilled out of one sack. And then the gold coins which poured from the other! Jack had never seen so much money.

He waited till the giant was asleep and snoring again. Then he crept out of the cupboard, snatched up the sacks and staggered to the door. He was terrified that the giant would wake up, but he was too full of food. So Jack made it safely to the beanstalk and carried down the sacks of treasure.

How pleased his mother was to see him safe! And she was amazed by the silver and gold. For three years, she and Jack lived happily and prosperously. Their house now had every comfort; they ate well and slept on soft beds. They had the garden enlarged, to include an orchard and a vegetable patch.

But it was still dominated by that huge beanstalk and, in the end, Jack just had to climb it again. His mother was against it and pleaded with him not to go. But the spirit of adventure was strong in Jack.

Besides, he had grown a lot in three years and he now had a beard, so he didn't think the giantess would know him.

He climbed the beanstalk again and went to the giant's house a third time. The giantess didn't want to let him in.

"It has always ended badly for us whenever I have let a human in," she said.

But Jack was a charmer and used to getting his own way. In the end, she let him in and fed him and then hid him in the copper. Shortly afterwards, Jack heard the giant coming home.

"Fee, Fi, Fo, Fum,
I smell the blood of a human one!"

he bellowed as he came into the kitchen, his nose twitching.

"It is only the pig I am roasting for your supper," said his wife. But the giant was still suspicious and hunted round the kitchen. Jack sat shivering in the copper, sure he would be caught.

At last the giant sat down to his supper and ate a

whole pig, and a cauldronful of jelly and custard. He drank a whole barrel of wine to go with it. Then he called for his wife to bring him his harp.

Now this was a magic harp which played the most wonderful tunes all by itself. Jack was enchanted by the sound of it and determined to steal this, too. He waited till the giant was asleep and snoring, then crept out of the copper and snatched up the harp.

But the harp, being magic, called out, "Master, Master!" and the giant woke up! Jack tried to run, but he was so scared he was frozen to the spot. Then he saw that the giant was too full to chase him properly. This gave Jack back his courage and he started to run.

The giant ran after him and, if he had eaten less, he would easily have overtaken him. As it was, he followed Jack to the beanstalk and started to climb down after him. Jack scrambled down as fast as he could, still clutching the harp.

He reached the ground and dashed to the garden shed for an axe, as the beanstalk was shaking with the weight of the giant. Jack hacked at the tough beanstalk with his axe and it began to creak and sway. Then it fell to the earth, bringing the giant down with a dreadful crash. He lay stretched out dead, taking up the whole of the vegetable patch.

Jack's mother was as glad to see the end of the beanstalk as Jack was to know the giant was dead. They lived happily in the same house for years and never lacked for food again. And Jack settled down and became just the sort of son his mother had always wanted.